165227

E
LAY
c. 1

Layne, Steven L.

Over land and sea :
a story of
international
adoption

ALICE GUSTAFSON ELEMENTARY LRC

506486 01361   30236B   0001   2-2012

Over Land and Sea

Over Land and Sea
A Story of International Adoption

By Steven L. Layne • Illustrated by Jan Bower

To AGS Readers

Steven Layne

PELICAN PUBLISHING COMPANY
Gretna 2005

To Victoria Grace, for whom I would travel over land
and sea again . . . and again.
—Daddy

And with great appreciation to Pam Gaston and the staff of Sunny Ridge Family
Center and Nancy Baker, Natalia Mashkova, and the staff of World Child
International for changing lives day after day.
—SLL

The word "Pelican" and the depiction of a pelican are trademarks
of Pelican Publishing Company, Inc., and are registered in the
U.S. Patent and Trademark Office.

Library of Congress Cataloging-in-Publication Data

Layne, Steven L.
   Over land and sea : a story of international adoption / by Steven L. Layne ;
illustrated by Jan Bower.
        p. cm.
   Summary: Two parents describe their journey over land and sea to find their child
and make it part of their family, as well as all of the joy and love the new baby brings.
   ISBN 9781589801820 (hardcover : alk. paper)
   [1. Intercountry adoption—Fiction. 2. Babies—Fiction. 3. Parent and child—Fiction.]
I. Bower, Jan, ill. II. Title.

   PZ7.L44658Ov 2004
   [E]—dc22

                                                              2003027658

Printed in Singapore
Published by Pelican Publishing Company, Inc.
1000 Burmaster Street, Gretna, Louisiana 70053

Everything in life has a beginning.

Fragrant flowers begin as seeds.

So do fresh fruits and towering trees.

Your family began with a seed, too.

A seed of love planted and nurtured in the hearts of two people—your mom and dad!

Across the miles, over land and
sea, your parents journeyed . . .

...driven by love, nourished by hope, and sustained by faith.

They came to find *you*
and bring you home.

ALICE GUSTAFSON
SCHOOL
LEARNING CENTER

Everyone celebrated your arrival. Friends and family came with food, gifts, and lots of smiles.

Of course, your grandparents visited the most, but who could blame them? You were their new grandchild!

Books, bottles, blankets, and bibs became part of a routine that included frequent trips to both the dinner table . . .

. . . *and* the changing table.

And in between there was peek-a-boo . . .

. . . and pat-a-cake . . .

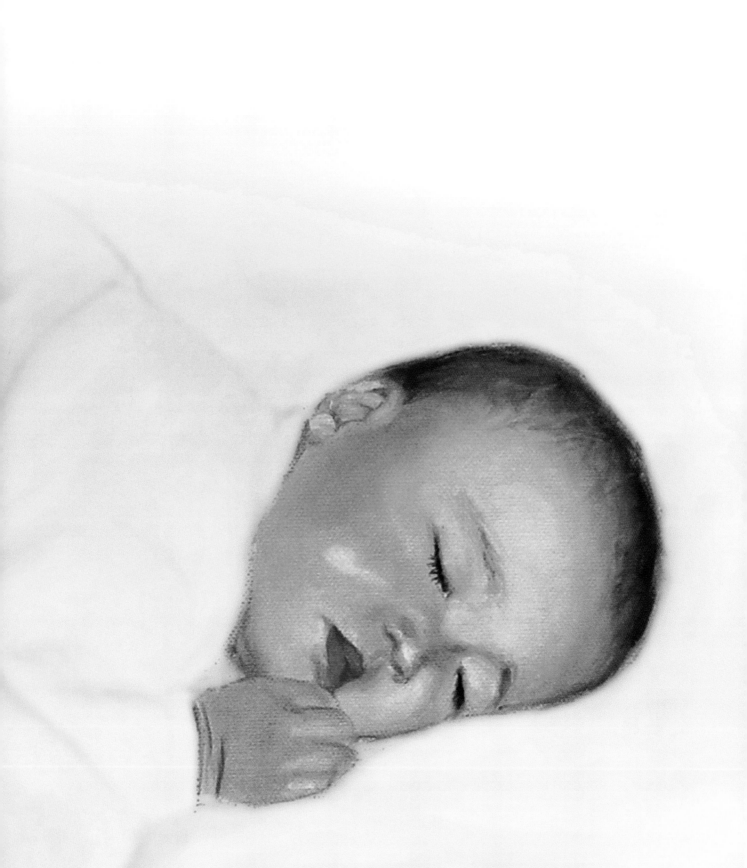

. . . and naps that were eagerly anticipated by the whole family.

Strolling in the sunshine,

playing at the park,

singing silly songs, and posing for
portraits took up a lot of time, too.

It was time well spent.

At night, in the quiet, Mom and Dad carried you off to a bed all your own. They tucked you in safe and snug, and then they prayed for your safety, for your health, and for your future.

They gave thanks, too, for the
unselfish love that . . .

across the miles, over land and sea,
changed their lives and yours . . .

... forever.

ALICE GUSTAFSON
SCHOOL
LEARNING CENTER